Let All Mortal Flesh

A.S.Chambers

This story is a work of fiction.

Historical characters appear in this work in fictitious situations. All other names, characters and incidents portrayed are fictitious and are the works of the author's imagination. Any resemblance to actual persons, living or dead is entirely coincidental.

First published in Great Britain 2016 by A.S.Chambers.

Copyright © 2016 A.S.Chambers.

A.S.Chambers asserts his moral right to be identified as the author of this work.

Cover art © 2016 Danka Lilly

ISBN: 978-0-9935601-3-2

DEDICATION

For Scruffy and Schroedinger - my furry friends.

Contents

ACKNOWLEDGMENTS

Once again, many thanks (and also, congratulations on her recent marriage) to Theresa Hughes for being a fantastic proof-reader.

Also many thanks to those establishments in Lancaster that allow me to lurk in a corner and sign a few books from time to time.

FOREWORD

Greetings reader! Thank you for taking the time to peruse this my third collection of short horror stories, some of which are dark, some quirky and some will have you rushing for the tissues. Now, I could never tell you which ones are which ("Spoilers, Sweetie!" to quote a certain River Song) but what I will say is this, by the end of this little book you will have a new-found appreciation for cats, dread ever catching a cold in our near future, wonder just what your neighbour cooked you last night and, hopefully, you will be eagerly awaiting my next novel *Sam Spallucci: Dark Justice* which follows on from the final two tales of Justice and Nightingale.

Oh, and the shadowy big bad of Sam Spallucci's universe finally gets to talk. Now, what was his name again? My memory is shocking...

FAMILY

The boy craned his neck to peer up at the young woman, her bright blue eyes framed by her short, dark hair. Her fancy clothes were so different to the ones that his mother used to wear. Whereas his mother's had been fashioned from fabrics that were mainly browns and greys and had consisted of more patch than original material, Nightingale's were fashioned from all manner of shiny cloths and were deep purples and reds.

"You like my clothes?"

The boy blushed and quickly studied his feet.

The sound of fresh water babbling over small, polished pebbles filled the room. The two other occupants gave a quick glance before returning to their hushed conversation.

Nightingale reined in her merriment and placed a gentle hand under the boy's chin, lifting his eyes back up to her crystal pools. "It's okay to look. I'm guessing you've not seen anything quite like us before? Well, apart from my rather dour older brother there."

The boy slipped a quick glance over to Justice, the quiet man who had rescued him from Salem just a few days previous. "About that..."

"What?" Flames from the fire danced in the young woman's eyes as she turned to prod the logs with a poker. The boy knew this was just for *his* benefit as the three adults had no need of the heat, being what they were.

Vampires. Undead creatures you saw pictures of in story books where they roamed the night, preying on the innocent. And yet, these three were nothing of the sort. They seemed to be on a mission, fighting other creatures, the ones made from clay. After the events in the alley, Justice had told him that those monsters were called *constructs* and served a dark master whose name and purpose was as yet unknown.

The boy's little world had suddenly expanded into a vast universe.

"You say that he's your brother yet, you don't look similar at all. You're all, you know, *pretty*," he felt himself redden again but carried on, "and he's so... so..."

"Serious?"

The boy nodded and the two of them chuckled conspiratorially in the pirouetting flicker of the fire.

"We're not kin like humans are," his new friend explained. "We just share the same father. He created us."

The boy looked over to the man that was talking with Justice. He was so tall! There had been large men in Salem: farmhands, miners, law-keepers. None of them, though, were the size of this individual. He was even taller than Justice and his blonde hair flowed like a waterfall down his back. Also, when he spoke, there was an unrecognisable accent to his tongue.

"And he is your king?"

Nightingale nodded. "That he is."

"So does that make you a princess?"

The water babbling over pebbles rolled into the room once more. "I guess it does," she smiled. "I guess it does." She leant forward and rubbed the material of his shirt between her fingers. "How long have you had this?"

The boy shrugged. "A while, I guess. I haven't gotten any new clothes since my pa died."

A cold finger stroked his cheek. "Well, I think it's about time that you did. Come on." She stood and the boy followed her to the door. "We're just going shopping," she announced to the others. "Won't be long."

The men watched in silence as they were left behind.

"Well?" the older man asked. "What do you think?"

Justice sat back in his chair, which creaked under his weight, and raised an eyebrow. "Of my new sister?"

His king and his father nodded slowly.

"She's certainly vivacious," he smiled. "Reminds me of someone."

"A certain Briton? Or perhaps her Trojan companion?"

The gunslinger smiled. "She has the tongue of one and the insight of the other." He pondered this for a moment. "A good combination, I think. Where did you come across her?"

"England," the older man said. "She was a maid in a large house, regularly beaten and abused by her master whilst being scorned and insulted by her mistress. Now she is free." He frowned when Justice made a small noise. "Something bothering you, my son?"

The younger vampire paused as he gathered his thoughts. This was his father and his king. He needed to tread carefully out of respect. "My liege, you say that she is free. How can that be truly so?"

"What do you mean?"

"Look at us! We are creatures doomed to darkness and shadow. You as much said so when you created me. When I cast my new eyes on my first moonrise you told me to treasure the moment as that would be the most light that I should ever encounter in my new life.

"Then you left me here."

The fire crackled as neither man spoke for a while.

"How can you talk of freedom," Justice continued, "when you, yourself, see yourself as nothing more than a slave? For heaven's sake, you even took that as your name – Doulos! You are a king who sees himself as just a servant."

"Mind your tongue, child." The king's voice was low but perfectly audible to his son's preternatural hearing. "You know why I chose my name. It reflects what I was and what I still see myself as. Just as yours is a snapshot of yourself. You are the lone gunslinger that roams this land, hunting down those that we seek in order to restore

8

our world as best we can."

"As best we can..." Justice's words were quiet, thoughtful.

Doulos knew there was meaning behind them and waited for it to be forthcoming.

"I sometimes feel that we are just jabbing pins in the coyote," Justice resumed after a while. "Rather than solving the problem, we just aggravate it with each blow that we strike. Yes, we remove the construct scourge one by one, but for each we cut down, two more rise. We should be blocking the source of the poisoned stream and not desperately trying to stem the relentless flow with our undersized fingers."

The king sighed. "You know why we have to do what we do."

"We don't know who has created these creatures," Justice nodded. "Aside from vague images some have seen in dreams and nightmares, we know nothing."

"That is correct. So we continue as we do until we find this monster and sever its head from its cancer-spawning body."

"But what of the others in this world?"

The fire spat and the king cocked his head in confusion. "The others?"

"The humans? What of them? Surely we should tell them of what we do?"

The king laughed deeply. "Really? You would inform these scurrying little termites that there is in fact an eternal war being fought in their midst by two races, both of which they would find abhorrent?"

"Not all would feel that way."

"No, but the majority would. They rule their peoples with fear and aggression. Look at this land which birthed you. The European invaders slew the indigenous natives in order to steal the very ground upon which they walked. What do you think they would do if they discovered that the creatures of their fairy tales were actually real?

"They would eradicate us.

"I have no time for them."

Justice frowned. His father's words were

harsh, spiteful. This disturbed him somewhat.

Doulos stood in one fluid movement. "Enough of this. Let us go out into the night and see what mischief your sister and your son are creating?"

The younger vampire rose to join the elder. "The boy is not my son. I have no desire to make him one of us."

"Really?" the king frowned as he donned his hat and his coat. "Perhaps, this is why you have such a soft spot for the mortals. I advise you to be careful."

"So, what about this then?"

All the boy could do was grin maniacally as words failed to convey just how stunned he felt. In the past hour he had tried on five pairs of shoes, eight pairs of pants, numerous shirts and three jackets. His brain was whirling almost as fast as the elderly shopkeeper who was struggling to keep up with his customers' every whim of fashion.

"Well?" Nightingale pressed. "What about it?"

The latest jacket was a deep royal blue,

almost black in shade. He had no idea as to what the material was but his fingers left tracks in the fibres as he stroked its soft surface.

The boy really liked it.

He nodded exuberantly.

"I think we have a winner!" the young woman declared to the shopkeeper.

The elderly man smiled benevolently, and with not a small amount of relief, as he began to bundle up the pile of clothes that his early evening shoppers had already chosen. "Will the young man want the coat packaging too?"

Nightingale looked down at the boy as he played with the fabric of the soft velvet. "I don't think we could part him from it if we tried."

The old man smiled and totted up the final bill. He did not usually open this late and had been rather cautious when the young woman had knocked insistently on his door, but it had certainly been worth it. No one ever spent this much. He handed the bill over and she placed payment on the counter. His eyes lit up at the bright, yellow gold.

"Keep the change. You've worked hard for it and that's appreciated."

The man let out a low whistle. Perhaps he would stay closed tomorrow and treat himself to a few whiskeys in the saloon? He bid the woman and her child a good night before locking the door behind them. As he slid the shutters closed, he did not notice the group of men fall into step behind his customers.

By the light of the moon, Nightingale smiled down at her young companion. He was rummaging through the parcel of newly-acquired clothes as they ambled contentedly down the street.

"Careful you don't trip," she said. "You should always look where you're going."

The boy raised his head, his grinning teeth bright in the light of the moon. "I've never had so many nice things. You've spoiled me."

"You're worth it. I know what it's like to have nothing."

"But you look all fancy."

Nightingale continued to smile, but this time the boy saw sadness in her eyes. "I wasn't always like this. I used to live a wretched life. My clothes were dull and tattered. I ate barely enough to survive. In fact, I was at death's door with a terrible illness when Doulos found me."

"How *did* he find you?"

The woman's eyes were off in the past as she continued her story. "He heard me singing. It was all I had left in life. I was so weak that I could not get out of my hard servant's bed. No food had been brought to me for three days and my pitcher of water had run dry. I knew that I was dying and it terrified me to the core. The thought that I would be left to rot in that miserable attic room caused me to dream nightmares of my wasted body dressed in a tattered nightgown. So I sang to myself to try and lift my spirits. My voice was frail, incredibly weak, but still he heard me. On my final night, the bedroom window slid open and he climbed in before bringing me back to life.

"Doulos saved me."

There was noise from behind and Nightingale snapped out of her reverie.

"There's no one here to save you now, my pretty." Three figures stepped out of the gloom. A strong smell of bourbon followed them. "Now why don't you just hand over those fine garments and some of your gold then we'll be on our way."

The boy froze on the spot but next to him Nightingale just sighed. "You don't want to do this," she said in a low voice.

There was quiet then a low cackle from the three deadbeats. "Really?" the pockmarked leader continued. "Oh, I but I think we do. You come into our town dressed in your fancy clothes, ordering our shopkeepers around and don't think that you'll have to pay for the privilege? Now hand the goods over!"

Nightingale shook her head. "No. We're leaving now." She placed a hand on the boy's shoulder and began to turn him away from the strangers. The boy then heard footsteps and another hand fell on his other shoulder. This one was nowhere near as gentle.

The next turn of events happened incredibly quickly.

One moment, one of the attackers was trying to drag him away; the next, the assailant was lying on the floor screaming, clutching at his arm which was now bent in a weird angle. The other two had drawn their guns and were staring ashen-faced at Nightingale who had positioned herself in front of their attackers, guarding her ward. The youth peered round her protective shield and looked up at her face then gasped when he saw what had caused the men to suddenly lose their nerve. A sharp pair of fangs were glistening in the moonlight.

"Leave us!" she hissed.

The two who still stood dragged their screaming conspirator to his feet and ran off into the night.

Nightingale and the boy watched them leave.

"Oh, we are in such big trouble," the young vampire finally admitted to the empty street.

They looked just like a pair of respectable gentlemen taking in the night air as they strolled down the main street of the western town. One wore an expensive frock coat, one a longer jacket of heavier, more practical material. Both were attired with wide-brimmed hats, suitable for keeping the sun from one's eyes on a long ride through the countryside. One sported a black cane that paced evenly as he walked. One had the unmistakable bulges of two holsters underneath his coat.

They looked as normal as normal did in this place.

Neither, however, possessed a heartbeat nor breathed in the life-giving air that sustained those who passed them. The heart of the one with the guns had stopped a few years previous and the heart of the one in the fancy frock coat had stopped many centuries before, when the world had been an entirely different place.

Different, yet curiously the same.

Technology had evolved, empires had risen and fallen. However, humanity remained ever constant: resilient, inquisitive and cruel.

Doulos had seen his fair share of cruelty. He thought back a few weeks previous to the sight of the emaciated young woman lying starving in her squalor. The reek of Death's cadaverous hand had been strikingly apparent when he had ventured into her small room. What remained of the cold, dead heart in his chest had fluttered with empathy and sorrow as he had watched her staring off into the unknown distance, softly singing to herself. He had only recently created a child. His first in his long, lonely years as a Child of Cain. He had never wanted to burden another with the responsibility with which he had been shouldered back in the days when the highest form of fashion had been a finely crafted sandal. For almost a thousand years he had walked by the side of his mother, a vampire who had seemed as old as time but was in fact just a couple of centuries older than himself.

Together they had wandered the shadows and the nights. The dull moon had been their waxing and waning guide in their hunt for the misshapen, insidious creatures of clay: *constructs*. They had needed to remain hidden, shrouded from the view of the humans who continued to be born, live their short lives then die. They constantly moved from place to place so as not arouse suspicion from their natural longevity.

Never could they put down roots. Never could they befriend those who they protected.

They were outcasts. Pariahs.

He had caught the vaguely hidden glances she had cast him which told of the regret that she had carried in creating a child to lead her people upon her end.

And end she did.

One night in some Mediterranean country, Doulos had come back to the house in which they had been lodging and had found the place empty. The room had been in turmoil, furniture broken, ornaments smashed, and there had been blood.

His mother's blood.

He had tracked her to the outskirts of the village, to a clearing where a huge bonfire burned bright in the darkness of the night. In its midst was his mother, bound to a stake and roasted to a crisp. The villagers looked on, jeering and cheering as they feasted and drank the locally fermented wine.

None of them saw the sunrise of the next day.

So, when he had seen this young dying woman lying, singing quietly as her life had ebbed away, Doulos had been torn. He had not been able to let this innocent child die. Her words had been so beautiful and had told of a spotless soul, one who cared for others and saw the good in those around her. He could not let that beauty pass from this world.

Yet, what was he damning her to?

And who was responsible for her state?

He had drawn close, mesmerised by her song, and without even thinking he had drained her and fed her with his blood from which she was to be sustained. Then, as she had slept and had been reborn, he had dealt with her employers.

Their screams still echoed through his ears.

Doulos' head snapped up as did his son's.

That was no distant memory. That scream was very much in the here and now.

"Trouble," he growled, and the two of them picked up their pace.

This was bad. Very bad.

"Quick, down here." Nightingale chivvied the boy down a side alley. Her first thought had been to return to the tavern and lay low until things had quietened down.

However, it appeared that their erstwhile attackers possessed a number of noisy friends and acquaintances. She pulled her young companion down behind some barrels, ignoring the stench of something rank and unmentionable, then waited for the horde to pass by, waving their torches and pitchforks or whatever it was that restless villagers used in these parts to show anger at things that they did not care to understand.

Nightingale frowned as she felt the boy quaking in fear and inwardly she cursed herself for her stupidity. "Just be quiet and they'll not notice us," she whispered reassuringly in his ear.

"We saw them come down here!" Nightingale recognised the coarse voice. It was the pockmarked leader of the little gang. "Split up and search the alleys!"

The boy froze next to her. This was not good. They needed a diversion.

"Whatever you do," she said in a low voice, "do not leave this place."

He looked up at her and her stomach lurched at the abject terror that dwelt in his young eyes.

"Stay here and you will be safe. I will lead them away and come back for you."

Nothing.

There were footsteps at the entrance to the alley.

"Please. Just nod. Anything. Tell me you understand."

The boy curled up in a ball behind the barrel.

That would have to do. There was no more time.

Nightingale erupted from their hiding place

and threw herself screaming down the alley. Three villagers were left flattened on the floor as she leapt out into the main street. Heads turned to face her and shouts of surprise followed as she ran away from the crowd. Not turning around, she listened to the sound of many running feet pursuing her.

She allowed herself a small smile as she played decoy.

Two shadows silently peeled themselves away from the side of an innocuous building.

"They came down here."

Doulos inhaled through his nose and grimaced. "I'm surprised you can smell anything over the stench of sweat and horse excrement."

Justice shrugged. "I grew up in this country. Certain things are just background sensations." He followed his father out into the street. Something was wrong, and not just the angry rabble that they had been both following and avoiding for the last hour or so. Doulos was distracted. There was a matter on the king's mind that the he was not sharing. "We *will* find them."

The older vampire nodded absentmindedly and walked off across the road.

Justice sighed quietly and followed. As he did, he was aware of another presence falling in step behind him. A quick mental dissection of aromas caused him to smile. "Greetings, sister."

"Greetings, brother," Nightingale replied.

Justice looked her up and down. "You seem somewhat dishevelled."

"Oh, you know. A late night run and all that." She grinned infectiously and walked over towards an alley which their father had just entered. "Let's get your ward and leave this place, shall we?"

"Agreed."

They both walked down into the alley and stopped when they saw Doulos peering down at some foul-smelling barrels.

There was no sign of the boy.

Nightingale screamed in surprise as she slammed into the wooden panelling that made up the wall of the alleyway. She felt herself hammered over and over again into the splintering material. In the background of her consciousness, she was aware of someone shouting, possibly at her, but things were exceptionally hazy.

Then she was free-falling onto the grimy alley floor.

Concentrating on bringing the surrounding world back into focus, she cautiously pulled herself up to her knees and looked up at an extraordinary sight. Doulos had gripped Justice by the back of his longcoat and was holding the gunslinger up above his head. Justice was ranting and raving, cursing harsh expletives which Nightingale knew instinctively were aimed at her. Tentatively, she stood up on her feet, leaning against the shattered wall for support.

"...kill her... untrustworthy... the boy..." Words started to prise apart the foggy clouds in her head and she began to comprehend what had happened.

"I'm sorry," she whispered. "I'm so sorry."

The raging vampire calmed somewhat and his father dropped him to the floor. "Enough of this," the blonde giant scowled. "What's done is done. We must leave."

His children stood and gawped as he picked up his hat, dusted down his frock coat and turned to exit the alley.

"No," said Nightingale.

"No!" shouted her brother.

Their father stopped and without turning back to them, said, "We cannot stay here. Enough damage has been done. We cannot save the boy without revealing ourselves. We must leave. Now."

There were two brief gusts of wind and he turned to view an empty alley.

"Plan?"

"Grab the boy. Leave."

"That simple?"

"That simple."

"What if anyone tries to stop us?"

Justice was silent.

Nightingale watched the growing crowd down below. The young vampires had taken the high route, silently leaping from rooftop to rooftop, providing themselves a wide perspective of the town. It had not taken them long to find the assembled lynch mob by the town hall.

The boy had to be inside.

"Well?"

"We concentrate on saving the boy then deal with anyone who gets in our way."

The young vampire could not mistake the steel in her older sibling's voice. "No one gets hurt," she insisted. "Promise."

The gunslinger's pale eyes fixed upon her. "If anyone gets hurt, it's your fault for not protecting the boy."

"Oh, don't you go pinning this on me!" she hissed. "And why do you just call him *the boy*? Why don't you use his name?"

Justice looked away quickly.

"You are joking, aren't you? You don't know his name?"

Justice pulled out one of his six-shooters and inspected the barrel of the weapon.

"Unbelievable! You drag him away from his normal life into ours, where the monsters under the bed are real, and you don't even bother to find out his name?"

"So," Justice said, still studiously inspecting his gun, "what is it then?"

This time Nightingale was awkwardly silent.

"Perhaps you asked him when you treated him like a doll, when you were dressing him up in fine clothes? Perhaps you enquired when he sat scared in the depths of a shit-smelling alleyway?"

The female vampire just glared at her brother.

"I thought not.

"Names are funny things to our kind, aren't they? They portray what we represent rather than who we are. Is it so strange that neither of us thought to enquire of his?"

With that he leapt down into the street, guns drawn.

The first bullet took out a kneecap of an old-timer with a shotgun. The second fractured the wrist of a stable hand who fumbled with a pair of ancient pistols that he had only ever used to shoot tins off a fence. The third went harmlessly into the air and caused the rest of the crowd to scatter for shelter.

Nightingale had to begrudgingly admit to herself that she was rather impressed. She caught up with him as he reached the door to the town hall. He had his ear close to the door. "I count twelve heartbeats, one beating almost twice as fast as the others." Then, before she could answer, his foot raised and kicked the door clean off its hinges, straight into the building.

Startled cries came from within along with the thump of two individuals being flattened by the imploding door. Four rapid shots felled four more of the mob. Nightingale sped through the gun-smoke and cracked the heads of two others.

That left three and the boy.

Two more shots. Two cries of pain. Non-fatal but excruciating.

One left.

The pockmarked assailant stood cornered in

the far side of the room. The boy was grasped in front of him, his eyes as wide as a mine shaft, his fear twice as deep. A sharp knife was clasped to his throat.

"Give us the boy." Nightingale's voice was calm, quiet. "He comes with us. We leave," she reassured the man. "No one has died."

The mortal's eyes flickered between the two creatures in front of him. They were devils. He knew that. They stood there, tall and handsome, not a hair out of place as if they were angels sent from on high, but he knew that they had come to drag him all the way down to the deepest, darkest depths of Tartarus.

There was no way out.

Nightingale screamed as the first drop of blood oozed from the boy's neck. The young lad's eyes seemed to fill his face as his heart beat galloped faster than a mail coach. She was aware of Justice taking aim and the gun exploding across the room followed by the insides of the killer's head decorating the wall behind him.

More and more blood soaked down the boy's blue velvet coat. The soft indigo mutated into a sticky purple as he slumped onto the floor, a pathetic gurgling bubbling up from his gizzard.

She leapt across to him and picked his limp body up in her arms. There was but one noise in the room of which she was aware. It was the dull pounding of a giant trying to climb an impossibly steep hill. Footstep after footstep became harder and harder as the incline increased. Slow and encumbered became his uneven gait until finally he stopped, sank to his knees and gave up on the futile ascent.

The woman who held the lifeless boy was incapable of words. He was gone. He had been here but now he was gone.

And it was her fault, her own stupid fault.

"Pardon?" She had heard something. One word but it had not registered.

"Leave," repeated Justice. "Go."

"Why?" she wanted to ask, but when she looked up into his empty eyes she knew the answer. She wanted to tell him, "No," but it would be a wasted word and words were precious. You never knew when you would say your last. Each and every one had to count.

Slowly, she lay the dead boy on the blood-soaked wooden floor, rose to her feet and walked out of the room leaving ten wounded men with her grieving brother.

It was a few hours before dawn when the family was finally reunited. The Children of Cain met at a cave far away from a town in stunned mourning. Doulos had spent most of the night there before being joined by Nightingale, whose face told him all that he needed to know.

When Justice arrived, the sky was seeping from black to indigo and the weaker stars were starting to fade. As he walked towards the cave, he watched his father putting the finishing touches to a huge bonfire.

The older vampire placed his last piece of wood on the pile and turned to face his son. "There is blood on your hands," he said.

"As there is on yours," his son replied. "Mine is just fresher."

Doulos nodded. "We are what we are."

"Killers."

The older vampire placed the last of the wood on the bonfire and pushed at it to test its stability. "That we are."

"What of her?"

Doulos looked towards the cave where his son's eyes were gazing. "I don't know. I really don't."

"You think that she is different?"

The father was silent, lost in his many thoughts.

"You think she will be a better monarch than me?"

Again silence.

Justice's worried eyes glanced at the pile of wood. "Talk to me. Please, tell me what you are thinking."

"I am thinking," Doulos struck a match and

tossed it onto the kindling of the pyre, "that I have seen too much death. I am thinking that I bear a secret that I can no longer hold. I could whisper it to the earth but the plants would tell all those that pass by. I could tell the sky but clouds would rain it down onto the people below. No one must know our secret, not yet. They are not ready. I cannot exist in this limbo any more.

"My child, I love you with what remains of my dead heart, just as I love your sister, but it is time for me to leave you now."

The flames pranced like plains horses in his pupils.

"But what are we to do?"

"I think you already know." With that, Doulos leapt up high and plunged into the midst of the funeral pyre.

All Justice could do was stand and watch in horror as his creator erupted into flames, like a dry cotton rag that had caught a stray spark. It was only as the fire burnt down and the ashen remains of the wood and his father fell in upon itself that he realised there was a soft sobbing coming from behind him. He turned and saw Nightingale, her face stained with blood.

"Why?"

"He could not carry on."

"Why did you not stop him?"

"I could not."

"What are we to do now?"

"You are to carry on."

"Me? What about you? Surely you are not considering…" Her eyes drifted to the dying embers.

Justice shook his head. "No. Nothing like that. I cannot be your king. I am not the right person to rule our kind. In his cold, dead heart he knew that to be the truth. That is why he created you."

Nightingale's voice rose an octave. "Me? Really? I think not. I know nothing. You are older. You have seen more. You are the first born."

"I am no ruler. I can live in the shadows but not with such a burden on my shoulders. I will do my part: furtively, silently. You will hear whispers of my deeds but you will not see me again.

"Not until the time is right.

"Our world is changing at such a rapid pace. People are not ready to know the truth yet of that which goes on right under their noses, but there will come a day when they *will* be ready — when they will accept that which they thought was fantasy is in fact reality. It shall be a time when I can stand in front of all the peoples of this world and tell them the truth. When that day comes, I shall return. Until then, I shall make sure that justice is served. I shall travel alone and follow my own path.

"Others of our kind will find you. They will see you for what you are, a kind, caring ruler. You shall be their Regent whilst their King is in occultation."

The first rays of the waking sun stretched their limbs above the horizon, crawling with searching fingertips across the plains. The siblings retreated into the safety of the cave.

"Justice," Nightingale said, "I am afraid."

"As am I," replied her brother, her King. "As am I."

MATILDA

It was hot. Unbearably hot.

Matilda lay sprawled out on the lawn chair in her neatly trimmed back garden. The sun blazed down and she closed her eyes against its searing rays. There was shade elsewhere in the garden, some trees provided a modicum of dappled shade over by the willow fence, but she could not be bothered to move. It required just too much effort.

She was getting old.

She knew that now and, more importantly, she accepted it. Not graciously, not at all. No, she despised the fact that her once sleek, youthful body was now no longer capable of the things that it used to be. No, she just lay out in the scorching summer sun, closed her eyes and glowered at all who came near her.

Matilda just wanted to be left alone. She had no idea how much longer she had left but she knew instinctively that the amount of days in front of her were far, far less than those behind her and she just wanted to be left in peace for the dwindling amount of time that she had left.

From time to time, visitors dropped by either for a perfunctory visit or just to be generally nosey, so she either turned her back on them and ignored them or made her feelings quite clearly known, depending on how her mood took her at that particular moment.

This was not how old age was supposed to be, surely? She had never really known her parents. Her father had never been on the scene and she had been separated from her mother when she was still very young. She never knew why. One of life's mysteries, like why did you have to pee so much more when you were in your twilight years?

When she was younger she could go for hours, now though…

Matilda let out a sigh. If her erstwhile lovers could see her now: frail, feeble and incontinent. Not like when she had been younger. She had had her pick of the bunch. She would wander round town, her head held high and take her pick of all the attractive males that tickled her fancy. Whoever, whenever, wherever: there had been no limits to her passions.

No children though. Funny that. Not once had there been a little slip or an accident. Perhaps she just had not remained with anyone long enough to really try for a family? Whatever the reason, perhaps it had been for the best? What sort of a mother would she have made? Imagine being knee deep in wailing, mewling offspring? The acrid scent of them constantly pissing themselves and the sickening noise of their constant petulance.

No, she would not have made a good mother. Not at all. Matilda smiled to herself. Thank heaven for small mercies.

Her eyes snapped open, her reverie disrupted.

She was not alone.

The birds in the trees that had been twittering so loudly had fallen incriminatingly silent. Something had spooked them.

Matilda growled under her breath as she scanned the garden with her failing eyesight. These days, anything as far as the willow fence was just a blur. Her sense of smell, though, was as sharp as ever and she took a deep breath.

The scent that hit her was unmistakable.

It was a young stud that she had known some months previous. They had undertaken a quick, torrid affair before he had disappeared and never returned. Apparently he was back and most likely wanting to rekindle their fire.

Matilda's fire, however, had been doused by the waters of old age. Perhaps that was why she urinated more these days?

The young male sauntered into the garden as if he owned the place. Some years ago, Matilda would have not let him dare. She would have challenged such audacity and chased him out with his tail between his legs. Now, though, she could not be bothered. She just rolled over on the lawn chair and presented the youngster with her uninterested back.

She felt a prod on her spine. Apparently he was not for taking a hint.

Matilda sighed her disinterest.

There was another prod.

Matilda turned her head to glower at the young upstart.

At least, she tried to

Pressure on her cheek pushed her face down into the cushions of the lawn chair and she felt a heavy weight mounting up onto her back.

This could not be happening!

Frantically, she urged all the effort she had stored in her aching limbs to roll out from under the mass of her unwanted paramour. She slid and snaked off the side of the chair onto the warm, freshly mown grass. Landing on her feet she stared at the intruder, venom in her eyes. He sat upright on the chair, looking for all the world like it belonged to him. For a short while they just remained that way, staring at each other: he young and cocksure; her, older and not wanting to enter into a fight.

Years ago, she would have lain the law down immediately. She would have swiped him across the face and left him bloodied for his audacity. Now though...

Now Matilda felt something inside her that had never raised its ugly head before. Fear. Her stomach was tense and her mouth was dry. She knew that he was far stronger than her and exceptionally agile. He could take her. He could pin her down. He could...

He could try.

She was not sure where it came from, but in an instant, Matilda was lunging up at the youth. For a split second she inhabited the body of someone far, far younger. Her legs pushed her up and her mouth opened in a war cry as she catapulted herself at the wide-eyed assailant. He cried out in shock as she hammered into his chest and barrelled him off the other side of the lawn chair.

They hit the ground with an almost silent impact. Matilda felt a sense of joy wash over her. The satisfaction that she had managed to pull of such a manoeuvre at her age filled her with pride. However it was a pride that was short lived when she went to pull herself up and one of her legs gave way to sharp spasm.

She cursed her age-wracked body as the youth rolled away and propelled himself forward once more. Matilda desperately tried to crawl away but something sharp slashed across her back and she screamed as she knew that she had been cut.

She also knew that she could not win.

She had to retreat. Quickly.

Clawing at the hard, sun-baked ground, Matilda frantically dragged herself out from under her attacker. She felt another sharp blow across her rear as she managed to scramble to her shaking feet and put as much effort as she could into bolting out of the garden which, if she were not successful, would become the place of her untimely demise.

She paid no attention as to where she was running. She just fled forwards, her legs working by memory of running alone. She had no strength left, just sheer determination to survive another day. Just one more day, a peaceful one, so that she could curl up and die in peace, not at the hands of a young, brutish rapist.

She looked neither left nor right as she staggered out of the driveway down the side of the house. She was too fixed on ensuring that her legs did not give way beneath her. She did not see the family saloon as it cruised down the quiet, suburban road. She was only vaguely aware of the screech of brakes then there was the excruciating sensation that everything in her body was somehow displaced.

The world spun around her. The floor momentarily became the sky until it rushed up to greet her in a painful, treacherous embrace.

Then there was stillness. She lay on the hot tarmac, her life ebbing away and she was aware of the sound of her front door opening and slamming shut, followed by frantic footsteps of someone running down the driveway towards her.

Then she was flying, scooped up into the arms of an angel. Water splashed her face and she tried in vain to lick it, thinking it would quench the burning agony.

And then there was nothing.

Nothing but a distraught woman cradling the limp body of her dead cat.

HUMBLE PIE

"My word, this filling is most delicious," Charles said to his sister-in-law. "It's a shame Josh couldn't join us for dinner tonight."

"Did you say he was away on business?" the effusive banker's perfectly manicured wife asked their demure hostess.

Angela thoughtfully rubbed the angry bruise on her wrist. "I'm not sure when he'll be back."

"Ah, well. You must give us the recipe,"

The quiet woman smiled serenely as she recalled the slashing of the knife and the screaming of her erstwhile bullying husband. "I'm afraid I couldn't do that," she explained. "It's a family secret."

SMOKING IS BAD FOR YOUR HEALTH

Abigail Smart looked at the time on her eco-friendly, self-winding wristwatch with a mixture of agitation and annoyance. "This really is quite preposterous," the middle-aged woman grumbled to her partner, Jeremy Whittaker, who was stood next to her, rocking back and forth in his cruelty-free walking boots. "All I want is a small packet of Golden Virginia and they can't manage to get the kiosk open on time."

Whittaker ran his smooth, office desk fingers through his bushy yet immaculately groomed protest beard. "Well, it is Sunday, Darling. Perhaps, they're not quite up to speed yet."

"Up to speed? Up to speed?" Smart shook her head so violently that her fair-trade Guatemalan earrings bounced angrily from side to side. "The wretched supermarket's been open an hour *for browsing*, for pity's sake. They're obviously trying to squeeze as much life out of their underpaid workforce as possible. That's the real reason."

She was about to launch into a pre-prepared lecture on modern slave labour when a young, brown-haired woman briskly approached the kiosk and let herself in behind the counter. The shop assistant was about to apologize for her tardiness when there was a commotion nearby. All eyes in the lengthening line of customers for the cigarette kiosk turned to watch an elderly woman in a dilapidated electric wheelchair skid her creaking vehicle into the front of the queue. She reached into a flapping handbag and slapped a screwed up ten pound note onto the counter.

"Weneee ee anayyy."

The young shop assistant's mouth mimicked the disabled woman's handbag as, in confusion, it too flapped open.

"Weneee ee anayyy," the elderly woman insisted, spittle dribbling down her chin.

"I don't believe it!" Smart hissed under her breath to her partner. To the woman who had pushed in front of her she said, "Excuse me, but we were first."

The old woman's rheumy grey eyes gave Smart a mere flicker of acknowledgement before she returned to waving the money at the befuddled shop assistant.

"Jeremy, did she just ignore me? Jeremy?"

Whittaker bent forwards between a melange of tatty bags for life that were hung from the wheelchair and tapped the old woman on her heavily padded coat. "I'm sorry, but we were here first."

The woman sighed. "Uh awwf," she threw over her shoulder before repeating her demand to the shop assistant whilst pointing frantically at the metal shutters that concealed the cigarettes.

As the assistant opened the shutters for the

woman to demonstrate which particular brand she was after, Whittaker stood stunned. "Did she just tell me to..."

"There must be a carer somewhere." Smart was craning her neck around to see if she could spot someone. "Probably some late teenage girl mooning over the glossy mags. Let's face it, *she* can't be out on her own. The smell alone suggests she's not able to look after herself." Her nose wrinkled and she whispered, "She pongs of wee, for pity's sake. Ow!" The perfectly attired woman jumped back as the electric wheelchair lurched back and ran over her foot before scooting away and out of the superstore, almost taking a display of lemons with it as it did so.

"Finally." She marched forwards before anyone else could steal her place in the queue only to encounter a crumpled hessian bag on the floor in front of the counter.

"Looks like she dropped her shopping," the woman in the kiosk commented.

Smart gave a deep sigh and bent down to

see what was lurking in the discarded carrier.

She peeled back a filthy-looking rag. "What on earth..."

Then suddenly there was a bright flash of light.

Matty Philips' ample stomach rumbled noisily from beneath his Millennium Falcon t-shirt. He just wanted to pay for the crisps he'd picked up, grab some *Rizlas* and get out. He had to meet his guy in about fifteen minutes and, at this rate, he was going to be somewhat tardy.

That was bad.

The cigarette kiosk was late opening up and there were a couple already in front of him: the bloke was some sort of hipster dude, judging by the beard that looked like it belonged on a guy from Lush, and the woman was so straight that you could use her as a guide for hanging wallpaper but she quite obviously wanted to appear hip to please the guy.

Perhaps he had a massive cock?

Philips' chuckled to himself

His mirth evaporated when an old woman zoomed her electric wheelchair into the front of the queue. She was funny looking: all grey and wrinkly under a huge overcoat and loaded down with shopping bags. Her head seemed to poke from the top of her coat without the aid of a neck.

"Weneee ee anayyy," the woman squealed at the shop assistant who had just arrived at the kiosk.

"Whoa, she's a lady Jabba!" Philips' chuckled. "Go on, say, 'Han ma bogay.'"

She didn't. Instead she repeated, "Weneee ee anayyy," and the woman in the kiosk looked mightily confused.

Philips' nerves started to get the better of him and his stomach rumbled once more. This was going to take forever! His guy was going to be so pissed off! He'd probably want more for the dope. The ginger-haired stoner rummaged around in the pockets of his barely washed jeans and found all that he had in his possession: a snotty hanky, various bits of fluff, a stormtrooper mini figure and enough cash for his usual amount of weekend fun. He was going to have to improvise. Perhaps if he grabbed something from the tech department of the shop on his way out, that would pacify his dealer? He looked up and saw the crazy granny snatch up a golden box of twenty *Benson And Hedges* before shooting off quicker than Han Solo flying the Kessel Run.

"Awesome," he smiled. All he had to do now was settle up here, grab something nice and shiny then head off.

Then suddenly there was a bright flash of light.

"Will you shut up?" Petunia Smith's son was, quite simply, doing her head in.

"I wanna *Freddo Frog*! I wanna *Freddo Frog*! I wanna *Freddo Frog*!" That's all it had been for what had seemed like the last hour but in reality had only been no more than sixty seconds. "I wanna *Freddo Frog*!"

Snot would be running down his face now. It

always did when he started to whinge. She couldn't bear to look at him; it made her feel sick.

"I told ya, they don't have any."

He continued on with his whining litany as Petunia looked forcefully forwards at the back of some fat, ginger-haired man with body odour issues. All she wanted was to grab her fags and get out of here. She'd smoked the last one on the way down and now she was gasping for another. To take her mind off her wait, she flicked on her phone and scrolled down her messages.

"Can't wait to see you."

"I want to rip your knickers off."

"I want to eat you up."

God, that sounded good! She shivered at the thought of strong hands undressing her and a firm mouth tasting her.

"I wanna *Freddo Frog*!"

"For the last time... You've gotta be kidding!" Some old bag lady had just barged her wheelchair to the front of the queue as the kiosk had opened. "Will you stop that?" Her son was yanking frantically on her hand as his lower lip stuck out in a pout. "Quit it!" Petunia pulled back, causing the youngster to trip over his own feet and collide with the man who stood behind them; the final member of the queue. "Now see what you've done!" she yelled at her son who was now starting to build up to one of his signature siren wails. This was too much. She should have left him at home with his waste-of-space dad who sat in his underwear and scratched his balls whilst watching the footie. She wanted to get away to the sender of her text messages; she did not want to be stuck in a bloody queue waiting forever for her cigs whilst some retard got there first.

Petunia looked up at the man behind them, the one whom her brat had clouted, and started. He was dressed in an immaculate grey suit and was clean shaven with neatly barbered hair. He would have been sexy as hell if he hadn't been looking at her son in a weird way. Reflexively she pulled her child close and his wailing stopped immediately. The man looked away from them and she followed his eyes as they tracked the bag lady hurrying out of the store, almost taking a display of lemons with her. His eyes darted to a tatty shopping bag that she had left behind and he half smiled.

Petunia Smith felt the deepest fear that she ever known.

Then suddenly there was a bright flash of light.

He waited at the back of the queue. There were five people in front of him: a middle class couple of seemingly bleeding heart liberals who were really as bigoted as Hitler's and Goebbel's love child, an overweight pot addict who was wondering if he had enough money to pay his dealer for his next fix and a self-obsessed woman who was not only cheating on her down-at-heel out-of-work husband but was also quickly regretting bringing her controlling child out when she really wanted to go and see her lover.

None of them were a threat to him.

He shifted slightly and felt the heavy weight

press into his left side under his precisely cut jacket.

Soon he would have purchased his pack of *Morleys,* be back in his car and driving out of this backwater town. He knew that he was risking a lot just for a packet of cigarettes (any one of the store's video cameras could pick him up) but he had driven for ten hours overnight and he needed that rich, roasted flavour.

It was the only joy that he had left in his life these days.

The bratty child was really playing his mother up. It kept crying over and over for a *Freddo Frog* chocolate bar. Did they still make those? All his mother was concerned about were the lewd text messages that her lover had sent her that morning.

He could make life far less complicated for her. One shot and the child would be quiet. Between the eyes, close range, no chance of missing.

"Weneee ee anayyy."

The man's eyes followed the commotion at

the front of the queue.

"Weneee ee anayyy."

An old, wheelchair bound woman was harassing the young shop assistant for twenty *Benson And Hedges* but, being rather inarticulate, was struggling to get her request across. Just another day in the life of the same old, same old.

Or was it?

The wheelchair was laden down with five battered hessian bags: four hanging to its back, the fifth in the woman's ample lap. The shop had only just opened, yet each bag seemed to be full to overflowing and dirty scraps of fabric covered whatever resided in the bottom of each bag. Clearly she had not just been shopping. Also, the bags were plastered with the logos of five different supermarkets. The one in her lap displayed the logo that adorned the wall above the kiosk that held his beloved *Morleys*, the others were branded with what the man guessed to be other local shops. As the woman leaned forward to point out her desired choice in cancer sticks, she took the bag from her lap and placed it at the foot of the counter.

The hairs on the man's neck jumped up, electrified.

Years of self-preservation screamed to him as to what was in the bag.

Then the boy of the cheating wife slapped him in the groin and his attention was distracted. It was so tempting: there was the boy, the gun was in his holster, seconds away from his hand.

Not a good idea. Not in public.

But it would sate the ravenous boredom.

As the woman followed her maternal instincts for once and pulled the boy close for futile protection, the man heard the clatter of produce as the wheelchair shopper darted out of the shop.

The bag had been left behind.

The middle class fraud woman bent to look inside.

The man smiled as he accepted that he would not be needing his cigarettes after all.

Then suddenly there was a bright flash of light.

Maggie pulled her wheelchair to a screeching halt. The lemons had been a close call, but she had steered around the display quite deftly. Now, outside in the car park, she fished out her phone, the one that had the oversized buttons suitable for her trembling fingers and punched the first of five speed dials that she had programmed that morning.

It was with great satisfaction that she watched the bright flash of light and heard the cracking explosion as the glass doors of the superstore burst outwards.

Giving a small grunt of satisfaction, she pocketed the phone, pulled the second bag down into her lap and set off into town.

She had a busy morning in front of her.

ARMITAGE

"Welcome, valued customer of Multinational Megabrand!" chirped the hologram of the pretty, blue-eyed brunette with the gentle hint of a Scottish accent. "We are pleased to inform you that your multi-purpose, sub-dermal, self-diagnosis device (version 5.5) is working at optimum capacity. As a result, it has diagnosed that you have a..."

"...*common cold*..." stated a flat, lifeless Home Counties male voice as the woman's lips moved ever so slightly out of sync.

"We have a hundred per cent cure rate for this illness, so," continued the perky female, back in time with her own words, "in no more than twenty standard minutes, a Multinational Megabrand patient service drone will arrive at your door in order to provide you with the relevant treatment. Please make sure that you are there to greet them. And don't forget to smile. Remember, a happy patient is a healthy patient.

"You have been charged fifty Megabucks for this message which will be taken from your personal savings account in twenty-four hours. If you do not pay within five minutes, the standard rate of sixteen point five percent interest will be applied at an hourly rate."

The face of the hologram morphed briefly into a frolicking unicorn with *MM* stamped on its shiny white arse before dissolving into the back of Armitage's hand.

"Well, that sucks," he said.

"What was that dear?"

Armitage glanced over at his cohabiting tax partner of thirty years, six months, eighteen days. She sat engrossed in the latest broadcast of *Jessica*'s yogalates exercise regime whilst crocheting a rainbow-coloured scarf that was growing snakelike over her protruding stomach. He moved their stuffed unicorn off the sofa and slumped down into the ageing furniture's overstuffed embrace. "I have a cold," he sighed.

His cohabiting tax partner of thirty years, six months, eighteen days almost dropped a stitch. *Jessica* didn't miss a beat, however. She just slid gracefully into the *unicorn's repose*. Armitage let his eyes follow the instructor's supple curves and toned physique. It would help soothe him from the oncoming barrage.

"You've got a cold?" his cohabiting partner of thirty years, six months, eighteen days screeched, her harsh, piggy eyes almost popping out of their weeping sockets. "Why on the Megabrand's Global Economy did you go and catch one of those?"

Armitage shrugged. "I didn't know I had one," he muttered. "I've not even sneezed."

The podgy fingers of his cohabiting tax partner of thirty years, six months, eighteen days resumed their fidgety twitching movements as the rainbow yarn started to knot once more in its precise, regimented pattern. "Just like you that is. Go out and catch a cold and not even know it. What am I supposed to do now?"

Jessica stretched a long leg up behind her slender neck and formed the *unicorn rampant* pose.

"Perhaps this thing is on the snark?" He tentatively prodded at the back of his hand.

"That's just like you, that is," his cohabiting tax partner of thirty years, six months and eighteen days, grumbled. "Blame everybody else but yourself. That's why you're still a domestic service employee. Bottom of the ladder, unable to make decisions.

"Not like your brother."

Armitage closed his eyes. Here it came.

"No, not like him, at all. He knows where it's at. All that rugby playing got him exactly where he should be — a chartered accountant. If it wasn't for the likes of your brother we would still be in that awful global financial mess. They swept through us like a dose of Multinational Megabrand patent bowel cleanser. They totted up the figures, worked out where the negative capital was and did away with it."

Jessica had taken a break for five minutes and an advert showed scruffy wannabe actors pretending to be homeless in a neatly manicured shopping precinct working together on making socks. "See how life is for the other side in our latest show: *Street Crochet!*" announced the slogan.

"And you know what the first thing they eliminated was, don't you?"

"Sick days."

"And what was the cause of most sick days?"

"The common cold." It was a mantra that Armitage had learnt all the way through his education at the local Multinational Megabrand Mind Academy. Illness was a weakness that threatened every civilisation. It prevented happy workers from undertaking their thrilling, worthwhile jobs and enjoying the great entertainment that Multinational Megabrand provided on every compulsory television in every room of every house that played on loop twenty-four hours a day (the enforced entertainment act had come into power shortly after the cure for the common cold). Once the common cold had been eradicated, there had been no more poverty or sickness. All those who had suffered from it had been cured.

Armitage thought about the cure. He thought about the Multinational Megabrand patient service drone that would arrive shortly and the infernally hot incinerator in its belly that belched fumes as it flew haphazardly through the sky.

He desperately wished that the adverts would end and *Jessica* would come back on. Her yogalates was so relaxing. Not like her previous show: *Tai Kwon Boxing*. That had been linked with a rapid rise in unfortunate groin strains so had been promptly axed after just six excruciating episodes.

Another ad was showing. Five quirky individuals talked secretly about each other's crocheted beanies and made humorous comments as they marked each other's efforts whilst riding home atop a luxury drone.

Armitage looked up at the five ceramic unicorns that frolicked on top of the television, their rainbow manes and tails swishing gaily with free abandon.

"You're just downright selfish," his cohabiting tax partner of thirty years, six months and eighteen days continued. "How will I survive without your pathetic, little income? Do you expect me to go out and work? I guess I should have seen this coming. My mother did warn me. She told me that I was spending the rest of my financial life with the wrong brother, but did I listen? No, I just ran off into the night on the whim of a young girl who had more romantic notions than... mmph... hummph... mmph!

Her berating words died into struggling gasps of breath as Armitage forced more and more of the rainbow coloured yarn down into her fat mouth. Her piggy eyes bulged as she struggled ineffectively to bat him away with her weak, wobbly arms. Armitage could not help but think that she resembled a unicorn vomiting rainbows. As his tormentor choked her last, *Jessica* gracefully resumed her show and slid into the *acceptant unicorn* pose, but Armitage had no time to watch right now. He had more pressing matters to attend to.

BING BONG!

The Multinational Megabrand patient service drone lacked the two things which would have made its existence that bit more bearable.

Arms.

BING BONG!

So it was that, rather than pressing the button on Armitage's house, it was instead playing the pre-recorded simulation of what it had been programmed to accept as a perfect simulacra of a domestic doorbell.

BING BONG!

Armitage felt his patented Multinational Megabrand fillings shudder agonisingly in his teeth as he dragged the lifeless corpse of his erstwhile cohabiting tax partner of thirty years, six months and eighteen days to the front door.

She was rather heavy so the task was slow and somewhat laborious. The task was also causing blood to seep through the bandage that he had tied tightly around his hand. It stung like a splintered crochet hook.

BING BONG!

Armitage finally reached the front door and elbowed it opens it with a breathy grunt. The giant behemoth hovered awkwardly before him. One of its rotors was spinning at a slightly slower speed than the others, causing it to list to one side. It was covered in dust and grime from the numerous chimneys that were arranged along its spine like a stylised dorsal fin. The industrial filth covered ripped and faded stickers that publicised other services of Multinational Megabrand and flickering video screens that looped trailers for upcoming crochet reality shows.

Plastered on the front of the semi-sentient automaton was the ubiquitous arse-branded unicorn.

Having nowhere else to really look, Armitage addressed the mythological mascot. "Good afternoon."

"PLEASE PLACE YOUR HAND IN THE SCANNER."

A rusted receptacle attached to a frayed cable tumbled out of the Multinational Megabrand patient service drone and clanked on the surface of the driveway. Armitage cautiously picked it up and slotted the hand of his erstwhile cohabiting tax partner of thirty years, six months and eighteen days inside.

"THERE IS A COVERING OVER THE HAND."

"She cut it this morning," Armitage explained. "Her hand slipped whilst she was crocheting a scarf. They were new hooks. Very sharp."

"ADJUSTING SCANNER TO COMPENSATE."

Armitage held the hand as steadily as he could whilst the Multinational Megabrand patient service drone fizzed, popped and whirred. Its faulty propeller stuttered and it lurched momentarily before righting itself.

"*THERE IS NO PULSE.*"

"It was a very deep cut."

The Multinational Megabrand patient service drone seemed to ponder this to the best of its limited ability before its neural time and motion interface relay decided that it was taking far too long on this particular job and prompted the machine to slide open its human-shaped receptacle.

"*PLACE THE PATIENT IN THE RECEPTA...*"
All the lights on the machine died, its rotors stopped spinning and the overworked bucket of bolts crashed to the floor. All the advertising screens flickered and went blue.

Armitage sighed, propped his rapidly stiffening erstwhile cohabiting tax partner of thirty years, six months and eighteen days up against the Multinational Megabrand patient service drone and walked around to the back of the machine where there resided a giant red toggle switch. He flicked the switch off then back on again and returned to the front.

Slowly, the machine growled back into life. The rotors whirred, causing it to limp unsteadily up into the air, cheerful music beeped and booped as the operating system on the screens rebooted before playing more adverts for crochet reality shows and the speaker coughed static.

"*YOU HAVE AIDED THIS MULTINATIONAL MEGABRAND PATIENT SERVICE DRONE BY TERMINATING AND REACTIVATING THE MANUALLY ASSISTED POWER INDUCER. PLEASE RECEIVE THIS FREE GIFT AS A TOKEN OF OUR APPRECIATION.*"

There was a loud popping noise as something dropped out of the belly of the beast.

"*THE TERM 'FREE',*" continued the Multinational Megabrand patient service drone, "*IS A TERM NOT COVERED BY CURRENT FINANCIAL LAW AND YOU WILL BE CHARGED TWENTY MEGABUCKS FOR THIS GIFT. PLEASE PLACE THE PATIENT IN THE RECEPTACLE.*"

Armitage grunted and groaned as he manhandled the flabby bulk of his erstwhile cohabiting tax partner of thirty years, six months and eighteen days into the large slot which subsequently slammed back into the Multinational Megabrand patient service drone. There was a large belch of smoke as its internal furnace began its work, then it lurched up into the air, gradually spraying incinerated remains from its chimneys as it did so.

Armitage watched for a moment as the machine lumbered away into the cloudy sky. When it was no more than a hazy smudge, he walked over to the free gift that the automaton had dumped on his driveway, picked it up and dusted it down. It was an entertainment disc entitled *How Yogalates Can Improve The Taste Of Your Coffee.* On the cover was *Jessica* posing in *suggestive unicorn.*

Apparently the day was getting better.

Armitage smiled and went back inside.

A.S.Chambers

MY DIVERGENT LAND

It's cold here.

I cast my eyes out through the fractured panes of stained glass across the barren landscape which has been fashioned by my own actions and I see rain falling on scorched earth. Not the warm, refreshing rain of spring that feeds and nourishes infant plants as they erupt from the warmth of their womb-like soil. No, not that. I watch as the cold, frigid rain of autumn relentlessly batters down all remaining life and foliage, forging it into a pulverised mess of decomposing matter and severed limbs.

The latter are the work of my children.

I close my eyes and listen as their viscous bodies shamble around my sanctuary in a lurching manner. They are my blunt instruments with which I fashioned this world to my liking. Before they rose from the ground, dragging with them the hatred of a cursed and abused planet, society was meaningless and frivolous. People would think nothing of spending a week's wages on a meal for two in a restaurant where the height of cuisine was a strawberry cut into thin slices served upon a smear of melted chocolate.

There are no such places now.

They have all gone, along with their pretentious clientele.

There is no place for them in my world, my divergent land.

You see, I grasped reality by the scruff of its flea-ridden pelt and shook it so hard that the blood-sucking parasites were eradicated and the future was changed. It had not been deserving of that which lay waiting for it – a time of peace and harmony. No, it had to be punished for what it had allowed to occur, for the decadence that had seeped insidiously through its veins like a powerful opiate in the bloodstream of a filthy, dirty, self-soiled addict. So I took it and smeared it across my very own fine china plate before carving up its occupants into delicate slivers, fine morsels and arranging them decoratively for my consumption.

I made a thing of beauty that no one before had been imbued with the talent to achieve.

But now, this perfect creation of mine is in danger. Forces dare to rise up against me. They battle my children and are emboldened by minor victories against my servants. They are led by an old adversary, one whose path crossed mine before I set foot on this, my blessed land.

He, however, cannot harm me and he knows it. He is not a man of virtue; for so it was said, "He who rose like a dragon of old shall be slain by the man of virtue."

No, he is a vile creature with a heart as dark as mine. He will rally his little band of warriors and send them to their deaths, laughing merrily as I wrench their final, gasping breaths from their bleeding, scabrous lungs. No one can touch me, not while I have my playthings in my possession, those items that saw the beginning of creation and remain forever eternal.

I am safe.

I am immortal.

I am Kanor.

VISIONS AND PROPHECIES

"Well this isn't exactly what I was expecting."

Nightingale tried her best to suppress a smile as she watched her offspring gaze around the small public house in a somewhat bemused fashion. It was on the corner of a pedestrian precinct in Sale, a commuter belt for Manchester. Not exactly what Dave had thought would be *vampire central.* "Really?" she asked. "Why might that be?"

"Is that a whippet sat next to the guy at the bar?"

"Perhaps it's a specially trained scout whippet?" She was finding it next to impossible to stop a wicked chuckle breaking up her words, but she was just about managing it.

"You have that sort of thing?" Dave's voice was a mixture of confusion and awe.

There was a despairing sigh from behind them and Marcus strode through the overly mundane room to a discreet door in a quiet corner. "She's playing with you," he explained. "We need to go through here."

Nightingale finally dissolved.

"Oh..." Was all that her offspring could manage before hurrying through the door that his mother's companion now held open whilst sporting a withering look of annoyance.

"Spoilsport," the diminutive vampire whispered to her smartly dressed companion. "I was only having fun."

Marcus looked down at his regent. "That's not what we are here for though, is it?"

Nightingale rolled her eyes and followed her child through the small door to the other world.

"Now this is more like it." Dave's eyes wandered round the back room. There was a long, highly polished bar that sported a number of gleaming pumps with a multitude of optics hanging behind on the wall. A white-haired, attractive woman winked at him as she methodically polished glasses. Some patrons were sat at the bar; a number were talking quietly in booths. Two, a pair of women - one sporting short cut red hair, the other long, flowing blonde locks - were dancing maniacally on a small dance floor by the juke box to something poppy and unmistakably eighties by *Wham!* The redhead looked over her partner's shoulder and caught sight of the three newcomers.

"Nightingale!" she shouted.

"Hey, Tigress," Nightingale called back. "How's things?"

The redhead broke off from her frenetic gyrating and walked over with the blonde. Dave glanced down and noticed that they were holding hands. "Oh, you know. Same old, same old." Her green eyes turned to Dave. "So you found him them?"

Nightingale nodded.

"Told ya! Scorp's always right. Aren't ya, babe?"

The pretty blonde nodded mutely.

"So, newbie? What's your name?"

"Oh, it's Dave. Dave Nichols," Dave managed.

Tigress raised a perfectly arched eyebrow. "Seriously? You're going with *Dave*?" Then, to Nightingale, "Where'd you find this guy?"

"At a comic convention."

Her brow still raised, Tigress eyed Dave up and down as if appraising a cheap *Primark* dress that had inexplicably found its way onto a mannequin in *Harrods*. "Well," she finally said, "At least he's not dressed like Spock."

Dave blushed.

Marcus sighed.

Nightingale sniggered.

Tigress' jaw dropped. "No way! She made you a vamp when you were wearing pointy ears?" Her laughter filled the bar. Eventually, when she had brought herself under control, she gripped her focus of fun by the hand. "Welcome to Vixen's Den. That's Vix over there," she pointed to the woman behind the bar who was watching them intently and pulled Dave close before whispering in his ear, "Just watch your pants. Maneater. Know what I mean?" Then back at normal volume, "I, as you must be aware by now, am Tigress, and this," she grinned, dragging her mute partner closer, "Is Scorpion." The blonde smiled bashfully. "She don't say much, well she don't say anything to anyone apart from me, but she's amazing."

Dave watched Tigress' green eyes fix on her other half and the flow of love from the brash redhead to the silent blonde was unmistakable.

"I believe that I sort of owe you my life," Dave said to the quiet vampire. "If you hadn't sent Nightingale after me..." His voice trailed off. "Thank you." He stuck out his hand.

Scorpion, shrugged an *it's nothing* and took the proffered hand of friendship.

Their palms connected then...

...everything changed.

The first thing that hit Dave was the heat, the blinding, scorching heat.

The second was the sun.

He cried out in fear and dived for cover. He was in a small street next to a large, stone building and threw himself behind some abandoned boxes and pitchers. It was no good, though. The sun still beat down on him and its insatiable heat licked every millimetre of his porcelain skin.

However, he did not burn.

There was no scorching of skin, no frying of flesh, no other combustible alliteration.

What he did feel was a hand slip into his. A slender hand, soft and feminine. He looked up at its owner and Scorpion smiled down at him. She motioned with her head and he followed her down the street of a city that was quite obviously situated somewhere hotter than the Manchester that they had apparently left behind. As well as the warm sun, there was the crunch of sand on the paving stones and a hint of the sea in the air. It was also somewhere very old. People walked down the street oblivious to the two vampires. There was no modern technology. In fact, there was no technology that seemed to have seen the light of day for over two thousand years. The citizens wore toga-like robes. Mules pulled carts. A small group of soldiers ran past carrying small shields and bronze-tipped lances.

"Where are we?" Dave asked.

Scorpion squeezed his hand and increased her pace, following after the soldiers. Dave accompanied her. They twisted through the rabbit warren of streets until they emerged at a large square by the massive gates of the city wall. Dave could not help but gape in amazement at the enormous portico that towered higher than many twenty first century buildings. The walls were truly impenetrable.

Then, when he walked out onto the beach before the city, he knew exactly where he was.

A massive wooden horse stood in front of

him.

"Okay," he whispered to his silent companion, "two questions. One, can anyone see us?"

He watched Scorpion study the inhabitants of Troy as they poured out of the city to view the massive equine gift. Not once did they pause to regard the two strangers in their unusual clothing. They just seemed to walk around them as if they were somehow guided around an unseen obstacle.

Scorpion shook her head.

"Right. Well that's good. So, next question. Why are we here?"

There was no immediate reply, not that he really expected one from the elective mute, however he noticed that she was gazing off into the crowd that was forming in front of the horse. He followed her line of sight and saw what was a small selection of citizens from the higher echelons of society. Their robes were made from lusher material and dyed in rich colours. Two women, in particular, stood out from the crowd. One was clad in a light blue gown and a gold tiara was threaded through her dark, immaculately cut hair. The other, standing next to her, stood out from the rest of the crowd, her hair a cascading waterfall of blonde in complete contrast to the surrounding roiling sea of dark locks. The blonde's lips moved as she turned to look up at the other woman and Dave felt Scorpion's hand involuntarily squeeze his.

"Well, that must be rather weird for you," he whispered.

The taller woman turned and said something to the other Scorpion before raising a hand and tenderly stroking her cheek then bending down and kissing her forehead. Dave afforded his Scorpion a quick glance and saw a small bead of blood trickle down her alabaster cheek. Unsure what to say, he snatched his head back to the women in front and studied the darker-haired woman.

She was the definition of beauty. Her glossy hair shone in the daylight and her eyes sparkled like the sea before them. The gown covered her body but was far from modest, it highlighted every curve and hinted at potential carnal pleasures.

This was a woman who was used to being worshipped.

Yet Dave found he could feel nothing for her. There was something about her that told a story of vanity and cruelty. He seriously did not want to be on the receiving end of her anger.

There was a commotion over by the horse where a bearded man was waving his hands and shouting to the staring onlookers. His tongue sounded familiar but not fully understandable. Dave heard glimpses of Latin but the inflection and phraseology did not ring true. However, the message of the man, as he ranted and screamed at the onlookers whilst gesticulating wildly at the horse, was obvious no matter what language you spoke.

"Beware of Greeks bearing gifts," Dave recited.

There was a murmur through the crowd, which seemed to be falling under the sway of the protestor. The man nodded and smiled at their response.

But then there was a commotion behind him. Something in the water.

People started to shout and point as the sea bubbled and rolled up onto the shore. They became nervous and agitated, anticipating some sort of ill. Then there was a rush of water up into the sky like liquid being poured out of a jug, but defying the basic law of gravity that would not be discovered for many, many years. The water spout coalesced and twisted into a serpentine form that spun and thrashed as if it were alive. It barrelled towards the shore and, at its head, a mouth opened.

Everyone screamed.

All except one. The dark haired woman watched impassively as the sea creature reared its head above the bearded protestor. All she did was wave her fingers in small movements by her side. She twirled them and the serpent twisted, she flicked them and its head swayed from side to side, she pointed them to the floor and it hammered down, its mouth swallowing up the unfortunate man before dragging him away into the ocean.

Then, as everyone else ran around in blind panic or fell to their knees begging forgiveness of the gods, she smiled, placed her arm around her version of Scorpion and turned to walk back towards the city that the next day would be in flames because of her actions. As she climbed up from the beach, she paused momentarily by Dave and his Scorpion and frowned. Dave felt his throat dry with fear and Scorpion held very still beside him, then the woman shook her head, took her ward and walked away.

Then...

...everything changed.

They were in a forest. Immediately, their senses pricked.

Fire!

There was the unmistakable stench of something sizeable and wooden burning out of control. An ominous smog of black smoke lazed its way through the dense trees. For a split second,

Dave thought he heard Scorpion gasp, then she was gone, darting into the black pall. He cursed, not wanting to be left behind and followed the quick flashes of her long, blonde hair that cast the occasional waymarker to follow in the gloom.

In a short while, he found her stood behind a tree, peering round at a clearing where a small cottage burned like a warning beacon in the dark. Off to one side, on the tree line, Dave could make out three figures. Two were bent over another who was lying cradled in their arms. Again, he could not fail to recognise the long, blonde hair of another Scorpion. There, with her, was Tigress. He did not recognise the man that lay in their arms.

Gently, he tapped his Scorpion on the shoulder. "You remember this?" he enquired.

The sadness in her face was all the answer that he needed.

The three were talking quietly. Dave tried to listen, but the roar of the blazing house masked their hushed words. Then the man's hand fell from Tigress' face and for a while there was no movement as the two vampires sat in silent grief. However, the tender moment of loss was shattered when an unmistakable scream of rage from Tigress cut through the forest. The redheaded vampire rose from the forest floor and rampaged around the clearing, shouting and screaming obscenities into the dark, annihilating anything in the cottage that had not already been devoured by the flames. The other Scorpion just continued to cradle the dead man, rocking silently back and forth.

Dave felt his Scorpion take a step forward. He flung his arms around her narrow waist and dragged her back. "No! No! We can't."

There was anger in her blue eyes with a heat comparable to the blazing fire as she frantically struggled to escape his grip.

"I'm sorry, I really am, but we can't interfere. Do you remember you being here? You can't change the past. It has dire consequences. There was this classic episode of *Star Trek*. Joan Collins was in it. Kirk and the others went back in time and... Ow!" He flinched as the struggling Scorpion bit his arm and broke free.

Dave threw himself forward and rugby tackled his time-travelling companion. Even as she fell heavily to the floor, she still didn't make a sound. He scrambled up her back and pressed his greater weight down on her smaller form. It was like trying to wrestle a cobra. Her lithe body rolled and undulated beneath him as her teeth tried to bite and slash at his face. Eventually, Dave managed to grab the back of her neck and pushed her face into the mud. "I'm sorry, for this," he panted, "I really am, but we cannot interfere with the timeline. We just can't."

Scorpion struggled a small while longer then lay ominously still. Dave tentatively leant forward.

All he could hear was plaintive, childlike sobs. Then…

…everything changed.

Dave felt a firm shove from underneath him and he rolled over onto this back. Scorpion pulled herself up to a seated position and slowly wiped her face clean. The two of them stayed there silently watching each other.

Inevitably it was the younger vampire that spoke first. "Why don't you speak?"

Scorpion's eyes flicked away from him and she doodled in the dirt with a finger before allowing him a nonplussed shrug.

An insolent rise and fall of the shoulders was better than nothing, so Dave decided to pursue the matter. "Back in Troy, you were talking to that woman. You were human then?"

A small nod.

Dave chewed his bottom lip as he recalled the woman's affection to his companion.

"Did you love her?"

Another small nod. This one almost imperceptible.

"Did she hurt you?"

Scorpion's eyes focused on the soil where she was doodling. A tiny drip of blood splattered the dry ground.

"She looked powerful. Who was she?"

Scorpion sent a daggered eye stab to her inquisitor that clearly said, "No more questions," before getting up, dusting herself down and walking off a small distance.

Dave rolled himself to all fours then up to his feet. As he did so, he looked at what the annoyed woman had been doodling in the dust. It looked like an upper case letter T with two swirls wrapped around it. He sighed. This was going nowhere.

Then he heard the unmistakable squeal of tyres and the sickening thud of a body hitting a car bonnet.

He felt chilled when he realised where they were.

They were behind a modern building, a huge concrete monstrosity which Dave recalled was a gym on the outskirts of Lancaster. He jogged quietly to the corner of the complex just in time to see the car that had just hit his former self squealing off into the night. Two figures tore across the car park of the hotel opposite and hovered over his broken body.

He knew this scene.

It was still fresh in his memory.

Nightingale bending over him, carefully tending to him. Marcus urging that they leave.

He saw his mother sink her teeth into her own flesh and offer her blood to him. He heard the noise of others coming out of the comic convention and the vampires were gone. Slowly, unsteadily, his former self staggered to his feet, groaned at the sight of his tattered *Star Trek* uniform and limped off into town.

There was a soft scuff of gravel next to him. Dave turned and saw Scorpion looking on in amusement.

"What?"

She reached up and tickled the top of his ears, giggling silently.

Dave could not help but smile too.

Then…

…everything changed.

Screams.

Screams everywhere.

Screams and the sickening sound of clay transforming shape.

Dave and Scorpion were stood on a plateau above what could only be described as apocalyptic carnage.

"Are those... angels?"

Scorpion nodded.

"They're not doing very well are they?"

Scorpion shook her head.

It was a massacre. An army of white-clad angels were being quite literally shredded by a horde of constructs. There were ripped wings and feathers being trampled into the bloodied ground and pierced bodies lay strewn across the field.

"What the hell is this?"

Scorpion's hand squeezed his and he looked up to a higher hill where another battle was taking place. Two figures clashed with swords, swiping ferociously again and again in an attempt to strike each other down.

"They really don't like each other do they?"

There was no response from his companion. She was staring intently at the two duellers. Recognition was on her face.

"What? What is it?"

Scorpion frowned then shook her head.

"Do you know those guys?"

Again the frown and a slight tilt of her head to the side.

Then one of the fighters flashed his blade forwards and the other screamed as his sword hand parted company from its wrist.

"Enough of this! This ends now!" The wounded dueller shouted.

Dave strained to observe what was happening. There appeared to be a bright light emanating from the wounded dueller then the top of the mountain was consumed in the brightest light that the vampire had ever seen. He and Scorpion bent their heads down, instinctively covering their eyes from the ferocious glare.

Then...

...everything changed.

More constructs.

More angels.

Another battlefield.

This, however was a different story. The angels seemed to be winning. They were driving the creatures of clay back. The winged warriors held up their hands and pulses of brilliant light flashed out, immobilising the constructs as if they were a Terracotta Army – glazed and polished, but ultimately useless.

Dave's brow creased as he watched the angels running in amidst their foes, smashing their solid forms apart and casting their desiccated remains to the wind. The sun shone high in the sky and baked the ground between the warring factions.

"Why did they not do this last time?"

Scorpion just shook her head. This was new

to her. He saw no recognition on her face, whatsoever.

And there, in the midst of the battle, one figure was claiming more construct kills than any other. Dave watched in fascination as a cowled figure danced and pirouetted between his foes, slashing left and right with a sword, cracking the air with a long whip which flashed silver at its tip in the bright sunshine. Not once could the vampire see the face of the animated fighter; some sort of cloth covered the fighter's face, preventing identification.

Yet, he knew him. He was sure of it. There was something familiar in this being's movements, the way he ran, the manner in which he leapt above his foe. It was as if the vampire had seen him before, in his dreams. As if he had run with him in the night.

Scorpion, too, was watching the battling stranger, her eyes locked on him in absolute wonder. Her mouth hung open at the grace and the ease with which he dispatched the constructs until, finally, not one remained.

"Claw!" Came a cry across the silent battlefield. "Claw!"

The being stood statuesque, his shoulders not moving the slightest from the heavy breathing that should have been necessary after such a feat, and raised his head.

"Claw..." The gnarled voice made Dave feel sick to his stomach.

He started as he realised that they no longer stood above the battlefield. Instead they were in a place which he had visited once before.

A place he knew that he would visit again.

The place where he would die.

"That is the name that you go by now."

There it was again. That voice. A dead voice. An old voice.

A familiar voice.

It was the church. The decayed, ancient place of worship that had been transmuted into a realm of death. Dave looked up and caught sight of the eviscerated remains of some unfortunate pinned to the ceiling. He tore his eyes away before having to look at the dead unfortunate's tortured face, before being stung by the agony written in bold letters across his visage.

It had been a gothic church. There were pillars of stone lining the nave and the remains of wooden pews rotted where once a congregation of the faithful had sat. At the west end stood a font, a stone dish for baptism. Around its rim was an engraving: "Knaves are not our responsibility." Dave frowned, both at the cryptic message and also at the noise that reached his ears. It was a soft singing, as if a shell was being held to his ear and the sea within was whispering a doleful lament. It called to him, wished for him to follow.

It was coming from the font.

It drew him towards it, held out its arms to embrace him.

Come to me, it soothed. *I am here. I will save you. Swim in my depths. I will make you whole again.*

He was oblivious to everything else: the hooded warrior who stood in the middle of the nave with his young companion behind him, the cloaked individual stooped over the dark altar at the east end of the church.

They meant nothing to him, whoever they were. He needed to approach the font. There was something there. Something which meant... What?

He did not know.

Come to me, the song repeated within his head. *I will make you what you are meant to be. I will tell you of such wondrous secrets. Listen to the marvels that I have seen.*

He found himself standing at the font as others discussed the fate of the universe. They were not his concern, not now, not yet.

He reached out, his fingers a hair's breadth from the stone of the bowl, and then there was a smaller set of digits in his other hand. His head turned and saw Scorpion holding his hand, her head shaking violently, but it was too late.

His fingers brushed the stone of the font.

And he was alive.

Not just a living, animated entity but truly, truly

alive. His heart beat and his lungs flexed as he inhaled the dank stench of death from the crumbling church, but it was so much more than that. Everything was there, it all stood before him, ready to be taken and understood. It appeared as water, wet and translucent, but it burned like the fiercest of fires. It was a ball of intense light, like the sun in the sky that would fry him to a charred crisp. It pulsed and roared in front of his mental self. All he had to do was open his mouth, inhale and breathe it in.

Yes. Yes. Breathe me in. Let me empower your atrophied lungs. You will see such wonders. You will talk of many marvels. Things that have been yet are still to be shall dance upon your tongue.

Be my messenger.

Dave made to inhale...

Then there was a scream.

His mental head snapped to the left and saw Scorpion there, still clenching his hand, her skin scorched and burnt. Her long tresses were aflame like the cottage that they had previously visited. Her eyes were melting in their sockets.

No! No! He had done this. He could not let her die like this.

"Save her!" He screamed at the watery ball of burning knowledge. "I know you can! I know that I will lose you, but save her."

Are you sure? Would you spurn my knowledge, my gift, to spare this other?

"Yes! Please, now!"

You are truly remarkable. There was wonder in the entity's voice. *I am not sure that many others would do likewise.* Then it undulated away from him and encompassed the burning vampire. It spread out into a blanket of light, enveloping her screams of agony, her torched body, extinguishing the flames and renewing her charred flesh until it was, once more, a supple pink. Her eye sockets opened and it forced its way into the small orbs that solidified again from their glutinous mess until they were once more bright blue.

And what a blue!

Like the vast oceans, they were the azure of sky reflected in the deepest waters that held the greatest of knowledge.

Scorpion opened her mouth and, instead of agonised screams, there were words.

Then...

...everything changed.

"He who rose like a dragon of old shall be slain by the man of virtue."

Dave heard the soft words from the unfamiliar voice and opened his eyes. There was the smell of polish, beer and concerned onlookers.

There was also a quiet murmuring of confusion.

"Did... Did she just talk?"

"I don't know."

There was the noise of someone barging through the crowds. "Scorp! Cassie! Are you there?"

Dave felt a soft squeeze of his hand and

looked over at the deep blue eyes that regarded him. "Thank you," they said without uttering a single syllable.

He squeezed the hand back and pulled himself to a sitting position.

"Are you okay?"

He smiled as he felt Nightingale's arm wrap around his shoulders. "Yes." He stretched his neck and felt his spine creak. "How long were we out?"

"Just seconds." Her eyes were pools of concern. "You just shook her hand then you both collapsed."

"It felt like a lifetime. I have a lot to talk over with you."

Nightingale nodded.

"It'll have to wait," Marcus' deep baritone cut across the hubbub of the room. "Look."

All eyes in the room shifted up to the widescreen plasma television on the wall where a number of faces, the likes of which you would not want to encounter in a dark alley, were being displayed. "In the following weeks," a precise female voice dictated, "more murders of known criminals have followed. Lancaster police…"

"Nightingale?"

The regent held a hand up for her son to be quiet.

"…have refused to comment on what local press are now calling the Vampire Vigilante."

The rest of the newscast was inaudible across the cries of disbelief in the bar.

"Nightingale. What is it? It can't be one of ours, can it? We don't do that."

Slumping down into a booth, Nightingale looked up at her child as she remembered words that had been spoken to her many, many years previous: *"When that day comes, I shall return."*

She looked up at her son, her companion, her subjects and words failed her.

Justice was back.

AUTHOR'S NOTES

Once again, many thanks for buying this little book of mine. I hope you enjoyed it. Here are a few little bits and pieces that I want to share with you regarding the stories.

Matilda.

I am fascinated by animals and I constantly wonder what's going through the minds of my two current furry companions. As a result, I went back to this little tale which I wrote in my twenties about a proud feline in her last few moments and I explored what she might be feeling.

Humble Pie.

I love flash fiction. The shorter the better. I originally read this out at Southcart Books in Walsall. It was enjoyed then. I hope you enjoyed it here.

Armitage.

I also enjoy the works of Philip K Dick. He influenced a story in my last collection and this one follows on in that same sort of vein. I constantly worry about the future of civilization as the growing power of elite multinationals snatch power away from ineffectual governments.

My Divergent Land.

Now, if you haven't read any of my other books, you will not have had a clue as to what this little piece was about. If you have, then hopefully I have whetted your appetite for more. The Divergence is coming…

Smoking Is Bad For Your Health.

This quirky little story almost did not make it into the

book. I had an abundance of material for this collection and the one that was supposed to go in (a Tigress and Scorpion tale) was just too long and will have to wait for the next collection. I'm not *too* sad as I love this little tale of standing bored in a queue.

Family. Visions And Prophecies.

So there we have it, the end of the six short vampire stories regarding Justice and his sibling, Nightingale. I have set the stage as well as opened a few windows into forthcoming books such as *Fallen Angel* and the *Divergent Land* trilogy (who is Claw, I wonder?). I have now brought the stories in line and ready to launch into the next Sam Spallucci novel, *Dark Justice*.

So, I guess I had better leave it there as my dog, Scruffy, is worrying about the builder in my bathroom and I really ought to…

What? You want some more?

Hmmm…

Oh, go on then. You can never have too much of a certain gun-slinging vampire, especially as he is now walking amongst us...

He couldn't breathe. The man's lungs dry heaved on the hot, stale air that resided in his mouth. He tried to scream, but his words came muffled to his ears.

There was tape around his mouth.

But not his nose.

Slowly, he took slow breaths through his nostrils. His lungs started to calm down, the heat dissipating as oxygen did its work.

Only then did he open his eyes.

Two other eyes were looking back at his. Pale, grey, dead eyes.

Barnes wanted to rip them out of their sockets. He writhed against the tape that bound his wrists tight behind his back and immobilised his knees and ankles.

"You can't break free," came the voice of his captor. "You're trussed tighter than a prize heifer at a rodeo." The man rose from his crouched position and walked out of Barnes' field of vision. Barnes struggled to manoeuvre himself around on the bare, wooden floor to follow the stranger. As he did, something else came into view.

The girl.

"She was innocent." Was that an accent? American? "Poor girl. What did you promise her? Riches? Jewellery? Perhaps it was fame? I doubt it was power." A boot connected with Barnes' chest and pinned him writhing to the floor. "Your type would never relinquish power. You thirst for it in all its forms. You suck dry those who possess it like a hungry leech in a stagnant pond. Once you latch onto the power you drink and drink, never full, always hungry for more. When your food supply dries up and dies, you just drop off and float away to your next meal ticket." The tall man bent over the dead girl and ran a finger along her cold flesh. Slowly, he sniffed the digit before running it over in his tongue. "Opiates." The word was low and mournful. "They ruined people in my childhood and yet still they flourish. I'm guessing you were cutting corners, mixing it up with something cheap.

"Something deadly."

In the half light of the shadowy room, the

stranger's pale eyes seemed to dance like small fires as he bent low towards his captive. "You have no idea just how worthless you are, little parasite. You swim from host to host, sucking away, happy with your lot, completely unaware of what is going on right under your nose. You see the wars on your television and just treat them like a game show. You hear of catastrophes around the world and think that they have nothing to do with you.

"You have no idea that the end is coming.

"But you can be of use. Yes, you can. You see, I have a purpose, a mission. Others will come after me but they need someone to pave the way for them, flatten the trail so that they can ride all the steadier.

"The world needs to know that my kind exist. It needs to be prepared and informed that we watch them, protect them." He leant in so close that Barnes could see each of his teeth clearly.

All too clearly.

"And you, my little leech, will bleed so very well."

The duct tape muted the screams that followed.

ABOUT THE AUTHOR

A.S.Chambers resides in Lancaster, England. He lives a fairly mundane life although, from time to time, complete strangers do ask him for directions to the nearest Post Office.

He is quite happy for, and in fact would encourage, you to follow him on Facebook, Pinterest, Instagram, Goodreads and Twitter.

There is also nice, shiny website:
www.aschambers.co.uk